We Are Wise,
Let's Hypothesize!

Kelly Doudna

Consulting Editors, Diane Craig, M.A./Reading Specialist
and Susan Kosel, M.A. Education

Published by ABDO Publishing Company, 4940 Viking Drive, Edina, Minnesota 55435.

Printed in the United States.

Credits
Edited by: Pam Price
Curriculum Coordinator: Nancy Tuminelly
Cover and Interior Design and Production: Mighty Media
Photo Credits: Comstock, Kelly Doudna, Image Source, ShutterStock, Wewerka Photography

Library of Congress Cataloging-in-Publication Data

Doudna, Kelly, 1963-
    We are wise, let's hypothesize! / Kelly Doudna.
      p. cm. -- (Science made simple)
    ISBN 10 1-59928-622-X (hardcover)
    ISBN 10 1-59928-623-8 (paperback)

    ISBN 13 978-1-59928-622-8 (hardcover)
    ISBN 13 978-1-59928-623-5 (paperback)
    1. Hypothesis--Juvenile literature. 2. Science--Methodology--Juvenile literature. I. Title. II. Series:
Science made simple (ABDO Publishing Company)

    Q175.2.D685 2007
    507.2--dc22

                                                                                            2006015231

SandCastle Level: Transitional

SandCastle™ books are created by a professional team of educators, reading specialists, and content developers around five essential components—phonemic awareness, phonics, vocabulary, text comprehension, and fluency—to assist young readers as they develop reading skills and strategies and increase their general knowledge. All books are written, reviewed, and leveled for guided reading, early reading intervention, and Accelerated Reader® programs for use in shared, guided, and independent reading and writing activities to support a balanced approach to literacy instruction. The SandCastle™ series has four levels that correspond to early literacy development. The levels help teachers and parents select appropriate books for young readers.

Emerging Readers
(no flags)

Beginning Readers
(1 flag)

Transitional Readers
(2 flags)

Fluent Readers
(3 flags)

These levels are meant only as a guide. All levels are subject to change.

A **hypothesis** is a statement about what you think will happen. The statement is your guess based on what you have observed. You test your hypothesis with an experiment to see if it's true.

Words used to talk about a hypothesis:

experiment
guess
idea
observe
statement

A hypothesis is my guess about why a crows.

I have observed
the 🐓 crowing
when the ☀ rises.

A hypothesis is my idea

about why 💧 is wet.

I think 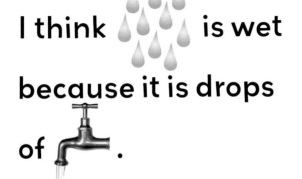 is wet
because it is drops
of .

A hypothesis is my

statement about why

my lemonade is

_____ .

My lemonade is _____

because it comes

from , which

are _____ .

We Are Wise, Let's Hypothesize!

Chris has an idea
that is the basis
for his hypothesis.
He thinks the ice cubes
will be done
melting more quickly
if they're in the sun.

I think that
the ice cubes
will change to water
faster where it is hotter.

Chris puts ice cubes on two plates to see if they'll melt at different rates. He moves one plate to the shade where he thinks the melting will be delayed.

I guess that when the temperature is lower, the ice cubes will melt slower.

14

Chris thinks he'll be right.
Soon the cubes
in the sunlight
have melted down
until there's only
water around.

The experiment
is through.
My hypothesis
is true.

15

We Hypothesize Every Day!

Tuan hypothesizes **that it will feel warm outside because it is summer and the sun is shining.**

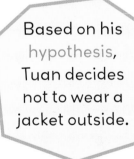

Based on his hypothesis, Tuan decides not to wear a jacket outside.

17

18

Inez has observed that watering indoor plants helps them grow, so she guesses that water will help the outside plants grow too.

Inez hypothesizes that the water will help the seeds she planted grow.

20

Liz hypothesizes that her new puppy, Wiggly, will play with a rope.

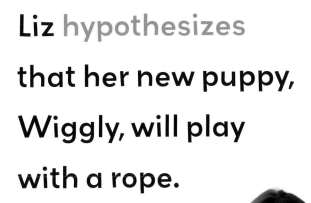

Liz remembers observing her old dog, Bart, play with ropes.

Rusty the dog is barking.

What is your *hypothesis* about why Rusty is barking?

Glossary

hypothesize – to make a hypothesis, or guess, based on a set of facts.

observe – to watch carefully.

shadow – the darker area created when somthing blocks the light from the sun or another light source.

statement – a report of facts or opinions about something.

temperature – a measure of how hot or cold something is.